The Halloween Witching Hour

Table of Contents

It was a brisk, fall morning when Sparta walked into her kitchen.

She cackled wickedly as she began her day.

"This is my favorite time of the year" Sparta said.

"I just can't wait for All Hallows' Eve" she said again.

Sparta immediately called her broom.

"Ronin come over here to me" Sparta said.

The broom immediately came out of the closet dancing all around the kitchen.

"Hello Sparta" Ronin said smiling.

"We need to go to the post office today" Sparta said to her broom.

"I must get the invitations out today."

"I have to invite all of my friends to the party that we are having on All Hallows' Eve."

"OK" Ronin replied.

"Hop on my queen" Ronin said again smiling at her.

She just laughed at her beloved broom.

Ronin had been Sparta's transportation for years and she absolutely loved him.

Sparta hopped on her broom then and she made her way through the Dark Forest.

She wanted to get to the post office to mail all off the invitations.

Soon they arrived at the post office.

Sparta was all excited as she slipped the invitations into the mail box.

Sparta knew that her friends would be here in a couple of days.

Sparta made her way back through the dark forest.

She was on a mission to have the most spectacular party of all time.

As soon as Sparta arrived back home, she hung up her hat and allowed her broom to go back into the kitchen closet.

Sparta was smiling the entire time that she was in her kitchen.

She began to boil her favorite brew for the party.

She could not wait until her guests arrived.

The invitations arrived the very next day.

One by one her guests received their invitation to Sparta's All Hallows' Eve Halloween party.

They were all excited.

All of the witches knew that Sparta threw great Halloween parties.

All of the witches could not wait to see one another.

They all got together only once a year.

Kita loved to go to Halloween parties.

She was the good witch of the North.

Kita began packing right away.

She put some of her new spells on her broom and began her journey to Sparta's house.

Kita just could not contain her excitement.

She smiled all the way to Sparta's house in the dark forest.

Lenore was the good witch of the East.

She had been around for years and years.

She even knew spells from the dark ages.

Lenore through a toad and a couple of bat wings into her nap sack and began her journey to Sparta's home in the dark forest.

Lenore flew throughout the night to get to Sparta's house in the dark forest.

She was so excited.

On the way to Sparta's house, she ran into a couple of bats.

"Hello there my pretties" she said to all of them.

The little bats just smiled as Lenore passed them.

Like Lenore, they also loved Sparta's parties.

Seeka was the good witch of the West.

She was so happy when she read the invitation from Sparta.

All the witches knew that she threw the best parties.

Sparta always had the best food prepared for her parties.

She spared no expense.

The witches knew that she created the best witching brew as well.

They simply could not wait for the visit.

Seeka began her journey to Sparta's house in the dark forest.

She called to her broom and laughed as she flew out the door.

"Ha, ha, ha" she exclaimed.

"We are off to the party" she said again.

Her broom just laughed at her.

Seeka was so excited that she began to do twirl around and around on her broom.

She got a little dizzy from the twirling but she did not mind.

Her broom began to cackle again.

The witches always got to see all sorts of cool things that go bump in the night.

They saw walking mummies.

They also saw feisty little black cats.

The little cats would screech and hiss something fierce.

The witches just laughed.

"Be nice little kitty" they would say.

The little black cats would just turn their backs and walk away with their little tails straight up in the air.

The witches would just cackle and smile as they road their brooms throughout the night.

The three witches knew they were close to Sparta's house in the dark forest.

She told them that they would pass a grave yard and they would have to make a right turn to get to her driveway.

Kita, Lenore and Seeka cackled with delight as they saw Sparta's house.

All the lights were on and they knew she was waiting for them.

The witches parked their brooms in the driveway.

The door to Sparta's house swung open.

"That's a new trick" they all said laughing.

The witches walked into the house and they noticed right away the table that Sparta had prepared for all of them.

They just knew that they were going to have a great time this evening.

Sparta came around the corner and she hugged each of the lovingly.

"Thank you for coming to the party" Sparta said.

"We would not have missed it for the world" they all said unanimously.

Sparta smiled.

They ate dinner, drank their punch, gossiped and discussed new witching spells while they circled Sparta's new brewing pot.

They all had a blast at the party.

The End

Sparta was the good witch of the South.

She loved the plan and have Halloween Parties.

She sent out all of the invitations and

She then waited on her guests.

Who were Sparta's guests?

What do they bring with them to the party?

Do they see anything that goes bump in the night?

Read on and find out for yourself!!!

Made in the USA
Columbia, SC
25 September 2022

67551922R00015